A City Happens in Love

A City Happens in Love

(Ishq Mein Shahar Hona)

RAVISH KUMAR

Translated from Hindi by AKHIL KATYAL

Illustrations by VIKRAM NAYAK

SPEAKING TIGER

SPEAKING TIGER BOOKS LLP
125 A, Ground Floor, Shahpur Jat, Near Asiad Village
New Delhi 110049

First published in Hindi as *Ishq Mein Shahar Hona* by
Rajkamal Prakashan 2015
Published in English by Speaking Tiger 2018

ISBN: 978-93-88070-60-7
eISBN: 978-93-88070-61-4

10 9 8 7 6 5 4 3 2

Typeset in Cormorant Infant by SÜRYA, New Delhi
Printed at Gopsons Papers Ltd.

For Nayana

Table of Contents

Our Growing World

The family of readers is only expanding. The publication of *A City Happens in Love*—translated brilliantly by Akhil Katyal—coincides with yet another reprint edition of *Ishq Mein Shahar Hona*. Since it was first published, this book has become a part of the huge world of Hindi readers and, now, I look forward to it becoming a part of the world of English readers too. And even as the number of readers has kept growing, I hope I've also become a part of your stories—those stories you remember, and those you tell. I'm grateful that this experiment, which first appeared in Hindi in 2015, has been accepted by you; and I trust that you will also accept it in its new avatar.

It is due to your curiosity and kindness that, today, everyone wants to know what it means to be 'Ishq Mein Shahar Hona'... and why there's no village in this book other than Delhi? It is questions like these, after all, that have made it possible for this book to become your own. Whenever you start filling any book with your own thoughts, or start searching for them within its pages, then that book finally becomes your own. A big thank you, for having made my book your own.

August 2018 RAVISH KUMAR
New Delhi

The City Becomes a Book

I have always seen the city from the lens of the village. Where people go and forget the village. The city came to my life as the city versus the village. Until then, the city was but a temporary address for me. In the column for 'permanent address' I always filled in my village address. Not where I had encamped in the city. On every occasion I found myself returning from the capital, Patna, to village Jitwarpur in district Motihari. All the time the difference between the home and the camp was intact. Home meant village, camp meant city.

Every time I returned to the village, a whole series of complaints was ready. The elders said it's only the village that is yours. It's your very existence. Know the village well. The city is only spoiling you. It's the village that will make you. That will save you. I too used to shield myself so that no one mistook me for a total city guy. I tried my best not to become the city. To become a city meant betraying the village. To betray the land that my ancestors had fed and watered. I used to be scolded by Babuji when I couldn't identify our trees and our lands. It seemed that the world around me wanted to keep me safe from the city but I, while holding onto the village, wanted to go discover the city.

On returning to the city from the village, all sorts of new rules about going out from the house were implemented. 'You have to return home before sunset.' 'No need to spend time with friends if they live too far.' I was allowed to go to the cinema only if I returned before evening. 'No late-night films; only those with a dubious character watch films this late at night.' 'Someone will steal the bicycle, or someone will run away with you.' In the afternoon, all the doors and windows were locked shut. It was like the Code of Hammurabi that everyone had to be back before Babuji was back. There was no such rule in the village. Which is why in my childhood I really explored the village. There, even that which belonged to others was ours, in the city, only what is ours is ours.

Maybe it had been my mother's sense of insecurity about her child being kidnapped in this strange city. Which is why she used to tell the story of the Gharkoswa child-abductors, who used to tie up children's mouths and shove them tight into gunny bags. Her fear was right though. They'd come to the city for the first time in her life. Once I was really young and had lost my way playing with friends. A huge search followed. When I wasn't back by the afternoon, Ma began visiting temple after temple.

Later, they found me at a Jain temple. I did not know the house address so that man at the temple had kept me there with him. Ma still offers thanks at that temple. She says, had it been the sadhus of today, they would've made you disappear. In the village, you cannot lose your house, but it can be lost in the city. Often in the cities, we lose our way returning home every day. The home itself goes missing.

Slowly, I let go of the ghost-shadow of the Gharkoswa story. Some afternoon, I'd turn into a strange lane or a neighbourhood. Only to see and recognize it as a part of my city. To figure out why this neighbourhood is different from mine. This habit of loitering began to make me be of this city.

Patna remained a mystery but I got to know many of its secrets. Behind the Gandhi Museum, under the shade of a peepal tree, I'd sit and gaze at the Ganga for hours. Hearing the voice coming from a boat far away gave thrill to my life. To free myself every time from the torture of failing the maths exams brought me to the quietness of the Ganga. These were the moments when, without letting anyone know, I began living the city. But every time I'd return home, the whole thing felt like no city was to be let into the house. We only lived in the city for the sake of the village.

Delhi taught me to be in the city for the sake of the city. But as soon as I got off the 'Eleven Up' train and saw the expanse of the city, I was shaken. I was afraid of Delhi from the very first sight. I'd seen in films how Dilip Kumar would come from the village and, right in the middle of the road, the city would bear down on him from all sides. Often I'd feel like this at the AIIMS crossing in Delhi. The DTC bus number became my new address. I recognized the numbers that took me home towards Govindpuri.

Slowly I began to understand that such a big city meant even more treasures than Patna! I began to do all that which I used to do in Patna. I began walking in the afternoons. I have travelled many lanes and neighbourhoods of this city during the afternoons. Just to look. The washing machines in the balconies and the women washing clothes wearing nighties or maxi gowns was the first scene that really became Delhi for me. Ghalib and India Gate came later. Before this, I'd never seen so many women roaming around in their nighties in the afternoons. Even though the nightie had arrived in Patna, it wasn't that popular. Had I been a painter, I would have painted Delhi on a nightie.

Friendship with Nayana transformed this city into a book. Rather, it transformed me for this city. We have loitered about a lot in love. That desire to say a little more before the goodbye made us walk miles. Delhi used to walk along with us. The fact that Delhi's a stranger is the best friend of romance. No one knew me or recognized me here like in the village. It's in these moments of love that I learned the historicity of monuments. I got to hear Nayana lecture for hours and hours on Mughal architecture. Yes, you have to study too, in love. You have to argue. We are not only defining ourselves but the city as well. Even today, when I hear the words 'lapis lazuli', time past begins to flutter its wings like a pigeon.

In my life however there was one other person waiting who carried a world full of cities with him—the late historian Parthasarathy Gupta. His lectures on urbanization that I'd heard during my MA days still act as a guide for me. We used to call him PSG. Something surely happened in his class which transformed Delhi for me into the Delhi of its people. Having left the Delhi of historians, I began wandering in the Delhi between Govindpuri to Bhajanpura.

One afternoon I went out roaming in an area near Bhajanpura. There were bras being made in every house. I saw male hands making bras for the first time. To see bundles and bundles of bras was like finally stepping out from inside into the outer world. I got so nervous that I almost ran back, meeting no one's eye. After many days, I went back to those lanes. I'd seen kite-thread being made, I'd seen steel being made at the Tata Steel plant in Jamshedpur. Even bras are made—this, I saw for the first time. Everyone should see a bra being made. Many people in their adolescence see only the body that is encased by clothes. To understand cloth as just cloth, one has to see it being made. Doing all this I became an advocate for a People's Delhi, not of the Delhi we find in the books. Delhi's not merely a coffee-table city.

So since then I've lived cities in many ways. Love makes better city-people of us all. We begin respecting every unknown corner in the city. We fill up those corners with life. Like during Chatth where I come from, we fill up the kosi. A circle is made of standing sugarcanes and then so much is filled within it. You explore a city from scratch only when you're in love. And to be in love is not just to find an excuse to hold hands. A lot keeps colliding in that space between two people.

'LaPreK'—Laghu Prem Katha, or Nano Love Stories—is the result of such collisions and efforts. To write 'LaPreK' on Facebook was to search for so much in that bounded space. Facebook was a new city for me. It was as if a breeze had carried a lot of people into my life. And like the first time, every one began discovering each other. Between all of them, I began discovering the city and began writing the 'Laghu Prem Katha' which Vineet Kumar and Girindranath Jha have taken ahead in even better ways.

When *Ishq Mein Shahar Hona* finally became a book, the first of the LaPreK series, I asked Sudipti scores of times if people would to like it or not. Maybe it is because of her trust that *Ishq Mein Shahar Hona* became a book. Sudipti's friend, Satyanand's guarantee did convince me, but I was still nervous. Thanks to Sudipti and Satyanand. And to Vineet too, with whom I kept checking if the literary community was going to take offence. In those days I thought about the book far more than I did while writing it.

Thanks to the team at Rajkamal Prakashan. Thanks also to their Managing Director Mr. Ashok Maheshwari who finally took on the responsibility of publication.

In fact it is the imagination of the Editorial Director of Rajkamal Prakashan that really kickstarted this book. It is Satyanand who thought about this book in so many different ways. Like a capable editor, he kept going to the extent of taking risks to do something new. If he hadn't believed, it wouldn't have been easy to say 'yes' to the book. Satyanand lives to do something new in the world of Hindi publishing. Hindi needs something new. Whether 'LaPreK' is the answer or not, it needs something new. A lot is happening, but the things being said are old still.

This book would not have been possible without Vikram Nayak. I have loved Vikram's work from the first time I saw it. So much that we then decided that we wouldn't meet regarding the book. Vikram should have the freedom to fill it up with *his* city. This book is Vikram Nayak's as well. Without meeting or talking, two people have written the same book together.

Thanks to NDTV India and its red mic that gave me the opportunity to see so many cities.

When my daughters grow up and read this book,

then my only wish is that they too find their own cities on their own. The city of Tinni and Tipu. May each of us have a city of our own, and may it be full of LaPreK!

15 January, 2015 RAVISH KUMAR
New Delhi

A City Happens in Love

A World City-like

I feel like a small town today...

And I feel like a metro.

You know, whenever you pass by South Ex, I feel like Karawal Nagar.

Shut up, you're crazy. In Delhi, everyone feels like Delhi.

That's not how it is. Not everyone in Delhi is Delhi. Just like everyone doesn't have love in their eyes...

Okay, but then how am I South Ex?

Just like I am Karawal Nagar.

You're right...

You know, if this Barahpula flyover wasn't there, then the distance between South Ex and Sarai Kale Khan wouldn't have shrunk so much.

Are you in love with me or with the city?

With the city; because my city is you.

This city becomes so empty at night, no!
It seems everyone has left it alone and gone somewhere. Come no, let us make this city laugh tonight. Let it not sleep at all. We'll either leap over the police barricades or get tangled in our own traps in the dark and fall.

Whatever you do, this city will still seem empty at night.

Why?

Because no one lets go of their loneliness just like that.

Saranga teri yaad mein... nain hue bechain... madhur tumhare milan bin... din katte nahin rain... vo amva ka jhulna... vo peepal ki chaanv... ghunghat mein jab chaand tha... mehndi lagi thi paanv... aaj ujad kar rah gaya... vo sapnon ka gaanv...

(Saranga, in your memory...my eyes are restless still... without your sweet arms...the day doesn't pass, nor the night will...the swing on the mango branch...the shade of the peepal tree...when the moon was in your veil...an' henna on your feet I could see...today all of it is lost... the dream we thought could be...)

Don't know why I'm listening to this song like some news slowly trickling in. Today this song feels like a Facebook status. As if someone was remembering the mango and peepal trees they lost long ago. Even forty years ago, nostalgia felt exactly like this. Village after village was being deserted. When this love song gives a little sigh of separation, it feels like a village being left behind. This was perfectly natural. Even though the villages settled the cities, they made the supply of memories so unending that no one living in a city ever gives comparisons for leaving a city behind. Like in your memory, the flyover over Moolchand seems so lonely, travelling in the metro so alien.

I'm only changing rooms. Not cities.
This Pushp Vihar room has all our memories and you say you're only changing rooms.
See, a tenant has no city of his own. There must be so many cities living in the lakhs of houses in Delhi. I'd found you on the terrace of one such house. Now only the address is going to change.
No, you're not an emotional man at all. I wish this city had a hem...
What would you do with it?
We would've made our room below that hem.

The rustling in the bushes in Nehru Park scared them both. From that clump of leaves someone with throbbing eyes was eating them up. Only two kinds of people try to find secluded places in Delhi—those who wish to love each other and those who wish to see people loving each other. In their nervousness, they got up so quickly that there was a stir in the nearby bushes as well. The lovers thought the police had come. He remembered what she said—what kind of a city is this? Always chasing the body!

From the Barahpula flyover—the back of Humayun's Tomb, the terraces of Nizamuddin, clothes drying upon them. As soon as she gets out of the car, she says, this place feels like being in between the roof and the sky; even at this height, it feels like that little ground wedged between Delhi and your love.

Removing the camera from the eye, I smile. Say only this—this bit of Delhi is just like relief, no? Just like you...

The sunrays began to recede as if someone was slowly drawing the window-curtain. Her orange sari caught the breeze coming from the Ganga. One hand on the railing and one in her hand. Their backs towards the Howrah Bridge. Thousands of people passing by. In front of them, the Ganga had become solitude. There was only one wall between the city and the river. Their backs. Letting their backs become wall, both drenched their dreams in the balcony of the Howrah Bridge.

Both of them liked being out on Delhi roads at dawn. As they reached the DND flyover from Sarai Kale Khan they could see a red sun over Okhla, and as they went down towards Ashram, she said—if only the Yamuna flowing below us had been alive, no?

He got a little bothered by this sudden, pretentious love for nature.

I have come all the way from Yamuna Vihar, I'm dead tired, and all you can think of is the river. How many cities will we move in this one city to look for a place!

They had met at the Chattarpur temple. But what they liked was sitting around in Jama Masjid. In the guise of soaking in history, a moment of seclusion in the present. After eating at Karim's, they would always climb up the minaret at the Masjid. Going up the narrow stairs, there was both the fear of watching Delhi from such a height and the consolation of holding each other's hands. It was this electricity of touch that was making them into city folks. After all, there aren't that many places in Delhi where you cannot but walk while brushing against each other.

The impatience to go to some new place and spend hours just looking at her brought us to Karawal Nagar. The exact opposite of Greater Kailash and its pretty homes, the place of desolation and half-way houses. Her beauty left uncovered by clothes caused a sensation in Karawal Nagar. Its people began to stare at her from the terraces and streets. Shit, where have you got me? We could have easily gone to those farmhouse roads in Mehrauli!

The crowds in the crammed Khanpur-to-Badarpur bus carried the two of them to a city where everyone except them was a stranger. With the push from the horde getting in at every stop, they were sent closer and closer to each other. Though the bus was running straight, they thought it was turning so rashly at each bend that they should hold the other to keep them from falling. Such corners for love come up on their own in a city. Even after being stared at in a crowd.

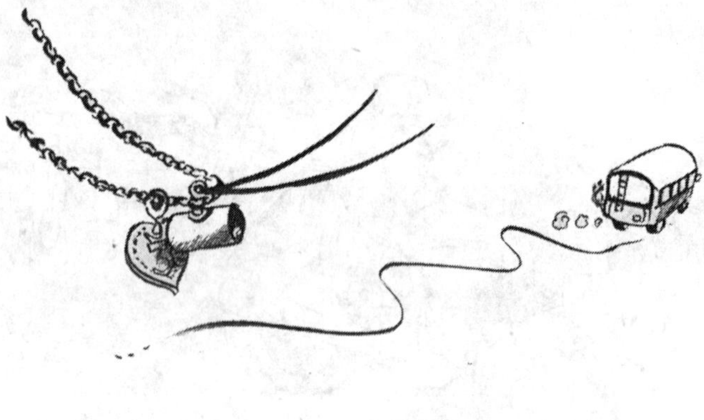

To escape the rain he parked the scooter under the Moolchand Flyover. They were so lost in each other they didn't even notice all the other scooters waiting around them for the rain to end. For no reason at all he kept trying to become her umbrella and she felt good under an umbrella she didn't need underneath a flyover. All the people around them stared as if they were a leftover piece of cloud...

Something or the other had been written on all walls. Every status had been stuffed with comments. Riding on a horse, he could be seen emerging from the rising sun. In this city beset by depression, every like seemed as sad as a dislike. The horse's hooves clanged on the pictures. Pictures of people resting in parks, resting in arms. Horseman. In this city of silent tongues, he reads the declaration of the death of words. Every word was shot and hung on the wall of statuses. In the close-up of the camera, the eyes of the horseman are brutal. This city is covered

by the corpses of words. There's no such thing which hasn't been said. There's no such corpse which hasn't been saddled with the firewood of words. It's only in search of a spark that the horseman kept running. This is a city of walls, sir. Here, a dead body of words is hanging on each wall—this voice drove him mad. The horse neighed. Lifted its legs. The horseman leaned backwards. Rose towards the sky. Millions of words were flakes now, flying in the air. Getting entwined with each other, making a network of sorts. The city...is getting buried in a dictionary.

To Be
To Be Together
Again and Again...

Riding sprawled like Spiderman, when he got off the metro at Anand Vihar, he was immediately surrounded by the claims of doctors who promise to restore manhood. Once his gaze escaped this, it meandered through the famous chaat shops, slid in and out of key-rings, over chole-bhature and all kinds of socks, finally alighting on that auto-stand, where she had come on time all right, but had forgotten to take off the mask of her dupatta. At that hour, several such masked girls had gotten off their autorickshaws. Several of them also passed by, pillion-riding with bikers. Skirting the rows and rows of Shikhar and Rajshri gutkha, his scream got lost in the hustle of Anand Vihar. Everyone, earpieces jammed into their ears, was busy climbing the stairs. Here, everyone was alien to each other. Mumbling, when he pressed the call button on his mobile, several ringtones of the same kind started ringing. In this era of the same sort of dupattas, the same sort of caller-tunes and earpieces, even our love is like Anand Vihar.
A chaotic, faithless, anarchic crossroads!

You show me dreams like flyovers do. You don't even realize that by the time you've climbed down the slope, those dreams will be stuck in a jam. Like the flyover at Medical, the dreams of flying like the wind vanishes by the time you come down on the Dhaula Kuan side.

Fine, but that jam at South Ex, surrounded by the shiny hoardings on the road, at least that looks like a dream, no?

Why do you always sulk like those old, yellowed government quarters in Sarojini Nagar?

Because you often seem a liar, like that Select City Mall.

He-he! Now here is the Barahpula and there Humayun's Tomb. If you say, we can climb down towards Defence Colony...

I don't know!

No road is completely deserted. Whenever you feel it is empty, someone or the other appears at some corner or the other. On Prince Anwar Shah Road a Pulsar bike appeared like this, suddenly. She was riding pillion, sitting on the higher seat, but was slumped over him like a load. Their helmets were bumping into each other. When the Pulsar stopped at the chai-shop, their pulse quickened. There won't be anyone here, no?

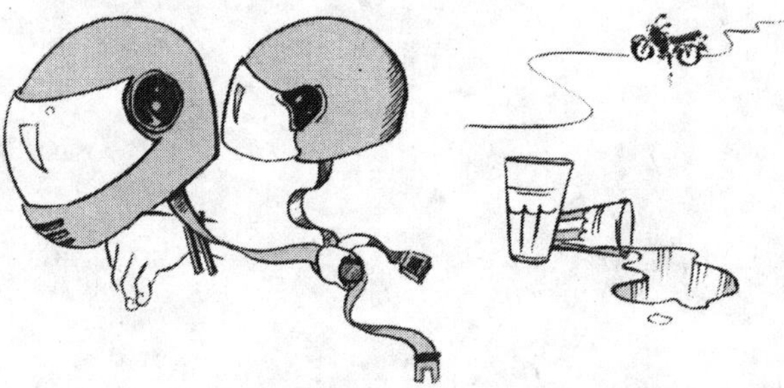

She'd just unfastened her helmet strap in style when someone stood in front of her. As if nothing had happened, as if no one had seen, she just went back and sat on the same seat. In such a style that even a Yash Chopra heroine wouldn't be able to imitate.

The guy also ignored the one who was staring. They just remained on the parked bike, talking to each other. When in love you don't just see, you learn to unsee too. 'Khepa re keno khunjish moner manush...'—the song was coming from some window. It meant—'O mad one, why do you search the heart of man...'

The metro suddenly transformed their lane. Unknown people began to come and go. Both of them changed their dream of a 10 by 10 room into a shop. And started roaming around Delhi on the metro in search of a safe place. She was locked in the ladies' coupe and he in the gents' one. Their journey was split up as if the Khap had turned up. Her complaints began to grow.

If we meet only after reaching somewhere and getting off this train, then why bother with the travel?

This is exactly what you don't get. There should be something in life that keeps whetting my desire to meet you. These days, I've begun to recognize you in the crowds of the Chitli Qabar Crossing even when I am standing on the height of Bhojla Pahari. It's not about the travel, it's about travelling on ways unknown to us. If we don't remain strangers in love, love itself won't remain...

Electronic meter. As though a certificate of his honesty. Chugging water from a Coke bottle wrapped in a black cloth, he kept saying—my earnings are not just out of hard work but also honesty. I go by the meter. How can I cut on honesty? Listen, if it's about reaching Lodhi Garden, then there's this curtain no, just draw it, it's for free. My auto does not have a back-meter. Standing behind me, she was blushing as much as she was getting angry. The autowalah kept on speaking. So-and-so used to travel in my auto. Now they even have kids. Do you know

So-and-so? They also used to go to Lodhi Garden in my auto. They are now fully settled as well. One day you will also stop coming to Lodhi Garden. Like them. Don't know why they stop travelling by auto after marriage. They don't go to Lodhi Garden either. Will you go? Or should I go look for another passenger?

It was March and the air had begun to heat up. Both of them insisted that the autowalah should drop down the flaps on both the sides. Even in the din of the auto, there was now an extraordinary silence inside. One of the driver's eyes got stuck on the rear-view mirror. To escape him, both of them began to hide in each other. The driver forgot the score of the meter. The auto began to race towards Shankar Road...

The metro has now linked Malviya Nagar to Model Town. In an hour, the hurtling train has cut quite some distance between the two of them. They now have time, but do not have much to say. All the plans that they'd made are now being outsourced. And along with this, the fun of thinking up things together, and doing them, was somehow fading away.

Yaar, you should come by bus, no...

Why? What's the problem with the metro?

At least I'll get the chance to call you and ask, where are you, when will you be here? We've become so unemployed in love. We don't roam about at all. How long will we just get off the metro and into the Mall to stick quietly to its pillars? Tell this metro to go away from here...

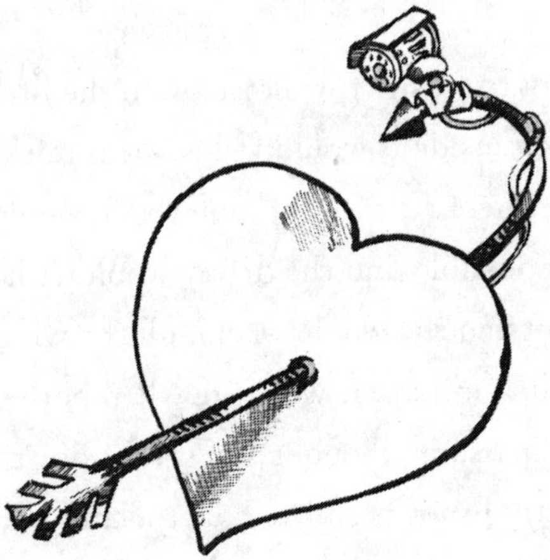

The buses of Delhi have changed so much, no!
Yes, the Leylands have turned into Marcopolos.
They don't move as much as they mislead.
How come you become so negative every time?
Arrey no, this is the only positive thing in this city.
What?
Marcopolo. If this bus wasn't there, where would you wander, where would we meet? Sarojini Nagar is full of CCTV cameras. Lajpat Nagar's the same. Every light in the city is caged within a camera. This loitering of the Marcopolo is good for us, Madam.
You keep taking the name of the bus, why not mine, Samar...
We're in the bus...someone will hear it.

If the auto wasn't this noisy, then the little bit of privacy inside it wouldn't last. This dark little room where we talk through touch wouldn't have been possible and the driver wouldn't have been driving, cursing the whole world, all the while looking into the back-mirror. It was rare when both of them had the exact same thought. He said, I don't get it, what exactly is not permitted, us touching or this auto-uncle staring back at us.

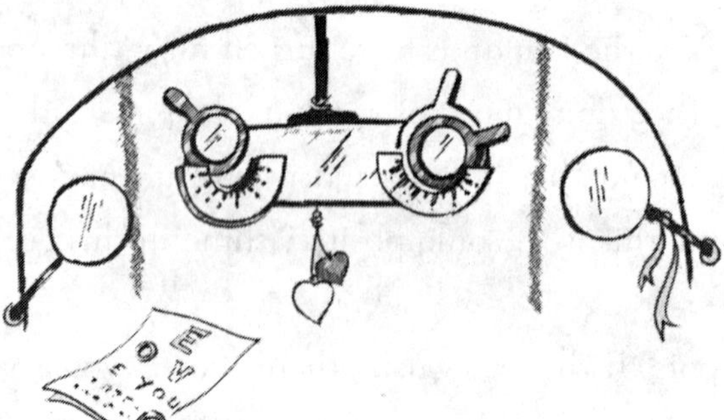

It's not about what's permitted or not, it's what you permit yourself, she said, look here, on one side Karishma aunty and on the other side mother

Aishwarya. Wonder who they keep looking at. We're being stared at from every side.

The auto-uncle was upset that the two were distracted by all this talking. Waiting for a good scene, he extended the trip. He turned towards the Ridge, maybe the road there would give the couple another chance to wrap themselves around each other, and for him to look on.

The elevated metro tracks of the Sector-18 market became their umbrella. She stood for ages behind those giant pillars. With the pretext of saving the bike from rain, they were saving each other from the eyes of the world. The parking attendant's dead stare from behind the pillar across from them broke their seclusion. Now they could hear the clamour of the metro passing above. The horns tore through into their ears. It had been difficult to find this one corner, and now these stares had turned it into a street crossing.

There was now the sound of the radio. Her car had turned from Dhaula Kuan and was racing towards AIIMS. She could not gather the courage to decide to return. Neither did he take a U-turn at Motibagh and come after her. While waiting for the other to come and console, both had gone too far. At Ghazipur now, and Ghaziabad ahead. And right after the Shiv-Murti, Gurgaon.

Love stories in the city are always like this. They start in traffic and then, in traffic, they are lost.

Love, Exam-Notes,
Loitering, Uff!

He was used to getting out the back door at night. A lover, wary of every little sound. Outside, he'd go and pass decrees on love and inside he'd lie at the feet of his beloved. One day, the beloved's hand fell out of his. Irked by this, she said, you claim my wishes are your commands and yet you fear my whims. Come, I'll make you my own and let the world know.

Once again, he tried to hide every little sound he'd make. He was about to explode with the tickling. He burst, saying, strange are the ways of love. I was taken by your eyes and am wounded by your ways.

Go ahead, let the world know.

Her Royal Princess came out and spoke, By my wish, he is awarded forthwith the title of the Beloved-of-the-Royal-Princess.

Now this particular ending of the play caused a huge uproar in the college. With this as an excuse, both of them went behind the curtains and wrapped themselves around each other. There's no better time to kiss than a ruckus.

Who's still awake this late at night?
The moon and the troubled.
And who's sleeping?
The sky.
Ha ha...when did you become a philosopher?
Since you became a lover.

Listen, I'll bring you the moon. Keep it by your pillow and lie awake at night looking for traces of the missing moon on Mall Road. I'll keep gazing at you while I fly towards Mars. How long will we keep dreaming of this Nehru Park and Connaught Place? Why aren't you saying anything...

What should I say, love is making you talk like a scientist. All this business of the moon is making you fall prey to a chemical reaction. Just because you see a Skoda car sitting in a DTC AC bus and sigh, doesn't mean that you can't see the moon in my eyes. Why make physics out of love?

Four steps at a time, the two of them keep going. Two hands are tied, two are free. The road under their feet keeps going on. Over their heads, the sky keeps passing by. Their sleep had broken because of the dhappp sound the Frooti tetra pack made when it fell on the leaves strewn beside the Hindu College walls. Why are we walking in the shadows of the walls, Samar? Why not this side, where the road's open.

But it doesn't work that way, my friend. In love, whichever way you walk, you'll be surrounded by the walls and their shadows. Even this sky, which seems like an open shade to you, actually it's keeping a watch.

Then Samar, am I in your eyes, or the universe's?

It's not like that...you are in my eyes, no doubt, but not hidden from the eyes of these walls.

At least you could have called me by my name...or is it that someone's listening...

Had it been anyone else, he wouldn't have gone to Nai Sadak and got a Champion Guide. He has decided that he will admit, this time, that his dream of becoming a lawyer won't get anywhere beyond Tees Hazari if he relies on cheap guide-books. She knows this but has never told him, the guide under your pillow has busted my illusion that you will ever become a Harish Dhawan or a Jethmalani after Law Fac. Even your dreams of Tees Hazari will remain locked up in this rented house in Anand Parbat.

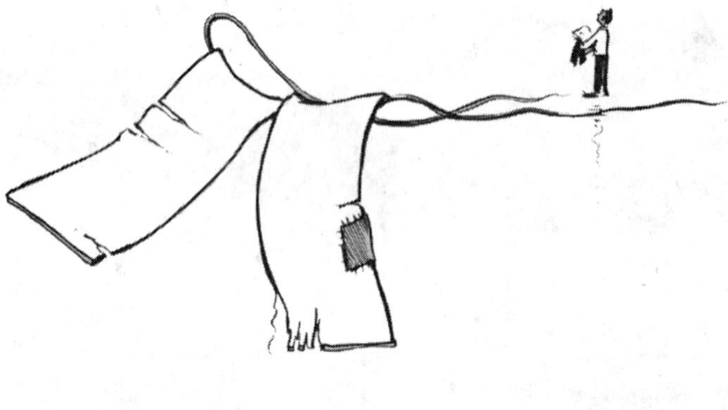

There was something about Dilli Haat. They would get lost together there, like lovers.

Yet, why was it that once they started walking down from Mall Road, they walked more like brother and sister as they reached Hindu College.

To go from familiar places to the unfamiliar is what it takes for the city to happen in love.

She used to say often—in France, people enter each others' arms right on the streets. You must get tired, no? Walking?

'Is love a crucifix? How do you choose those who love you?' She fled this song from *Saat Khoon Maaf*. She got out of Maitreyi College but, instead of heading to Najafgarh, she hurried towards AIIMS. It is difficult to save yourself from the Khaps of the 360 villages which grip Delhi. She took this restlessness within her to the winding flyovers of AIIMS and there danced like shrapnel. Dhaula Kuan is already a terrifying place...

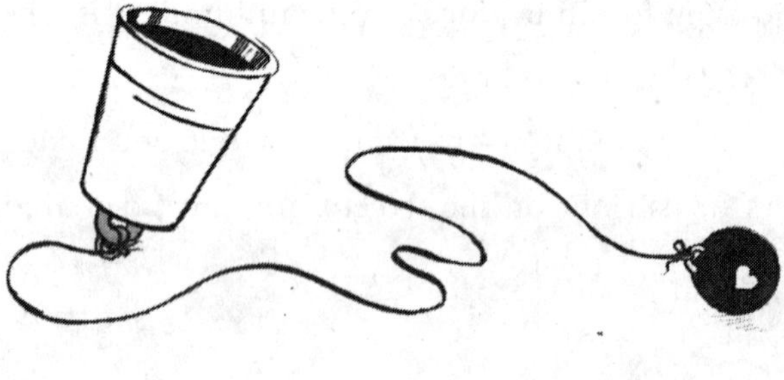

Couples on foot are often jealous of couples in cars. The insane dhinchak music from the cars coming out of Khalsa College and the girl sitting on the front seat. By the time he'd walk to Mall Road, he'd write a thesis on the side-effects of being rich. Economic disparity changes the meaning of love. What would the car owners emerging from Khalsa know of the love of those below the poverty line! Just going to Kamla Nagar and having ice-cream at Chacha's is not the only test of love.

He must have gone to make an ass of them... Leaving his annoying friends, he'd walk every day at 4 p.m. towards the P.G. Women's Hostel. Outside the hostel, while talking about life, land and love, he'd keep shoving Marxism in. Sometimes he would say he's a landlord from beyond the Ganga and sometimes he'd claim to be dirt poor.

If the girls of Delhi did not have so much stamina for listening, these migrant heroes from U.P.-Bihar wouldn't have had a chance in hell to be con artists!
As soon as it struck five, every time, she'd say—It's all very confusing...but very interesting!
He would return happy.

It's nice no, the multiplex has changed the very meaning of the morning show.

Otherwise just getting in and out was tricky. See, now I can hold your hand. Let Akshay Kumar jump around as much as he likes. This moment, only you and I are in this hall. And a few more couples like us. That's it. Thank god for the empty chairs.

Why do you always seek me out in the dark?

This one question turned the cinema hall into a police station. He went out to get coffee.

They found the corner seat at the back of the Minus Mudrika. She rested her head on his shoulder. When sleep came and when the bus, passing through Sarai Kale Khan, Ashram, Dhaula Kuan and Wazirabad, reached Jubilee Hostel, he didn't even know. Was she lost in thought or sleeping, he didn't even figure that out. He was busy clashing with all the stares that came her way.

As she got down, she was right when she said—you worry less about me and more about the world. You could have at least held my hand under the bag. Coward!

After that day, she could often be seen loitering about in Mukherjee Nagar. After stealing the notes from her, he had changed his flat. By now, she was bound by habit. Every room in Mukherjee Nagar seemed dark and she would peer in with the light of her love.

But he was in a room in Hakikat Nagar now, mugging from her very notes. He had decided. He wouldn't be a lover when the PT was around the corner. On the wall there was no picture of a heroine. There was a time-table. There was his father's dream...

It's 'just friendship', he'd tell his friends. She's not like that. He would start explaining as soon as they met. The two of us went to Arts Fac. To meet the Head. In the Central Library looking for books together and climbing up to its terrace for a cup of chai. Delhi University has no better place for chai than this.

Some relationships are like that, new places emerge for them. All sorts of excuses start being made. She knew it. He was not like that. It was he who'd hadn't quite figured out that he was exactly like that.

With the key kept behind the window, she unlocked the door and went in. Looked at the room with a detective's eye. Found all those letters in his case. The guy who couldn't keep even one of these many relationships, why has he saved all their letters! Baffled by this, she wrote a letter and closed the case.

'I am going. If possible, save my letter too. You'd know this—all these girls in the past write better than me. I have written badly on purpose.'

Listen, swear by the traffic jam at Ashram. Swear by that footbridge under which you hid to save yourself from rain. In the dark of the Moolchand underpass, you'd held my hand, swear by that. At Dilli Haat, you had ice-cream from my spoon; at China Bowl at Dhaula Kuan we were so lost in the sayings of Confucius; as soon as we would reach Mall Road from college, it seemed as if Delhi's courtyard had opened up for us. I have only one plea—do not ever let our love let go of this city.

A Little Like Yours, A Little Like Mine

He fell for the girl selling momos in Lajpat Nagar. So far he'd seen the seven-sister states of the North East only on a map. To stroll here every evening had become a habit for him. Secretly, she started giving him one extra piece for every plate of momos. After she smiled once, he began to say, it's very nice, each time he'd leave. After seeing Shahrukh's *Dil Se*, it seemed to him that this one extra momo was paving a new way for love.

He'd eat and he'd pay. The Lajpat Nagar aunties weren't bothered by this North Indian boy standing around this North Eastern girl's stall every evening at four.

Cultures can meet only in a marketplace. He just made one blunder. In return for momos, he gave her a thekua from back home one day. That was the last evening of him indulging his taste for momos...

These days, you've become the History Channel. History Channel, what are you saying?

Of course. Everything you say, your statuses and these places. Is this any sort of place to come to? Underneath the giant tomb of Humayun. Ruins, forts and tombs make love wish for walls before it even has a chance to grow. Don't we seem so helpless here? Then where should we go in this city! Why don't we see others here anymore? Even the shade of all these trees seems so empty no, darling?
That's why I'm saying. Sometimes, like MTV, we should just live in the present of the city and the cinema. Let's go to Select City Mall. That last pillar on the third floor, from where we came back on seeing that couple. Is it so important to write our names on these walls? If tomorrow's theirs, today belongs to us.

The Rajkumar, astride a horse, was riding along Rajpath. The sound of the horse's hooves rose and moved towards Raisina Hill. At Dhanteras, he had bought a steel tiffin-box and told his Mistress of Malviya Nagar that this was all that the Mumtaz-es of present day were fated to receive. The moon risen in the sky was competing with the glow of its made-in-China duplicates on earth. The dust rising from the horse's hooves drumming on the ground was hurting his eyes worse than ever. Untying her long hair, she did try to shield him from the wind, but her fingers sliding over her ears entranced him.

The Rajkumar declared—when we have nothing left, we will keep the two rotis of love in this tiffin-box.

Since the Mistress of Malviya Nagar came back from watching Formula One, she has been paying no attention to the Rajkumar of Raja Garden. This is precisely the tragedy that befalls these Hindi-medium princes. They are never really at ease with their English-medium girlfriends. The Rajkumar of Raja Garden was shouting himself hoarse at the sight of all the empty burger plates littered about there. He called Sachin and the guard cars useless. Remembering the country's farmers, he found the speed of his horse superior to all else, you know, considering the environment and such. The Mistress of Malviya Nagar merely said this was 'cultural difference' and turned her face away.

In all this anxiety, the Rajkumar of Raja Garden started reading Lohia. The Mistress of Malviya Nagar lost herself, intoxicated by Schumacher and Vettel. Sighing deeply, she said, India has arrived, Raja Garden has not. We can't meet. I love Grand Prix Noida.

This deep-brown bindi and the black sari with that huge golden border makes you look like such a type. The pencil going right through that hair-bun and the cigarette-smoke, it seems like it's someone else, not you.
So what, I like dressing up like this.
When did I say that? Just that whenever I see you like this here at India International Centre, it seems you've just popped out of Dilli Haat and landed here.
Uff, so useless, all your Sudhir Mishra, *Hazaron Khwaishein Aisi* type of comments.

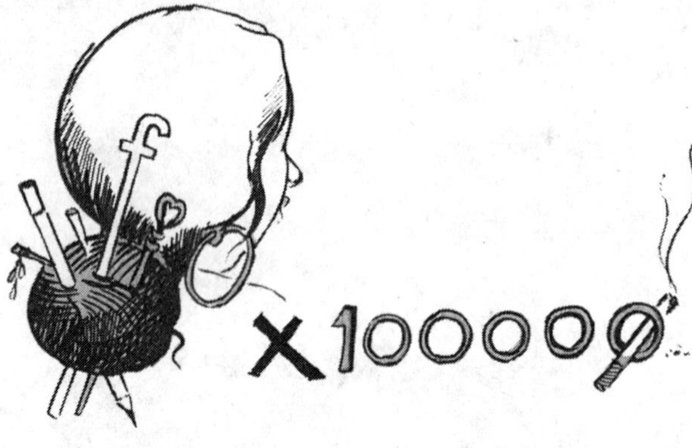

I don't know, people stuffed into such clothes have started looking fake to me.
Shut up with this nonsense. These statuses you keep writing on Facebook to spread consciousness, even that is copying someone else.
Who is original in this world? Even this love between you and me, who knows how many millions it has happened to, before us...

Bengal has long since left behind the Bengal of Jibanananda Das. If outside the Pujo pandals the joys of biryani, Dominos, mutton chops and phuchka still remain, that's because everyone has decked themselves up like billboards—stunning girls and good-good boys. In this collectivity of the festival, why is the drummer seen on the sides? Those who call themselves Rishidas—they know that they're from a Scheduled Caste, but do not know that reservation can change lives.

Arrey, leave it, yaar! How come you're seeing the festival through the lens of all these questions? Here, look, how am I looking?

Haan, you're prettier than the moon and more beautiful than Bengal.

Don't make fun of me. Why can't you see that, despite everything, the Baul tunes still remain and so does Rabindra Sangeet. Otherwise how would you have met me, if I hadn't been dancing in the Pujo and you hadn't been sitting in the front watching me. 'Holud chaapaar phool...aine de aine de...'

The urge for sea-fish took them both to INA Market. Parked the Pulsar bike in the corner, held the helmet by one's side and entered the market. The fish-seller understood—someone's come having read a cookery book. This is what irked her. She began to speak in English on purpose and he, putting the helmet down, began to examine the fish. When he turned around, he saw that an entire entourage of memsahibs had come stomping into the market. Ah, this is why you started off in English. Not every fight over status has to be fought with English! Chill...dear!

Should I say one thing? When I pass by Jor Bagh on your bike, then I feel like the seeds of our dreams are strewn all around here and one day they'll grow up and turn into a house. Lodhi Garden right opposite. Khan Market nearby...
See here, what's wrong with our Rajouri Garden!
I'm not living with you in Delhi's own Bulandshahar.
Don't forget it was you who put this dream in my head.
Darling, we'll also have a house like this... like this... this...Dream a bit no, yaar...

Listen, can't you take a house in South Delhi?

Why?

M Block Market seems so happening.

No!

What no yaar! You've become very negative. All our friends are in South Delhi. And here we are, setting up house in Rajouri Garden.

So what? There is no relation between love and place.

There is. South Delhi feels like my own. Like what I want to be, it feels like that.

I wish there was only one direction in this country—South!

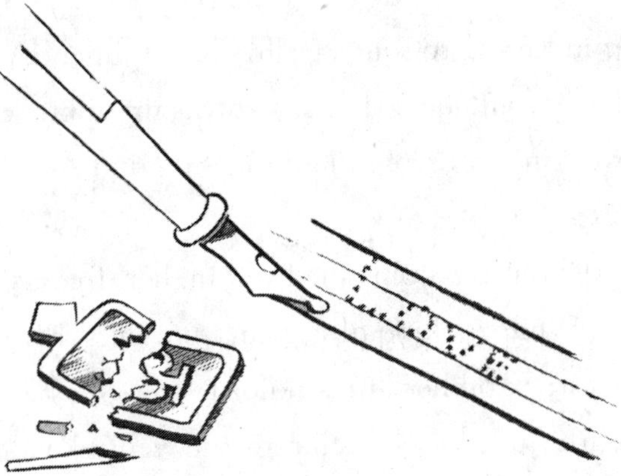

What a nice poem—Sabse khatarnaak hota hai, hamare sapnon ka mar jaana... (The most dangerous is the dying of our dreams) While drinking beer at Pebble Street in Friends Colony, she popped the question—why is Hindi poetry not popular? She started praising Vikram Seth and Chetan Bhagat to the skies. Why don't you write in English?

I know it but not that well.

Come on. You can write. If you'd written that Paash line in English, you'd have gotten the Booker by now.

She wasn't really damning him or anything but he started damning himself.

From Kerala to south Delhi's Sarai Jullena;
in that village of Jaats, a township of nurses
working in Escorts, Holy Family and Apollo
emerged.
Just like the rented rooms she lived in, her dreams kept changing. While looking after heart-patients, her own heart was stuck on her last landlord's son. She began to love Sarai Jullena so much that she went ahead and opened up a dhaba—Malabar Hotel.
Besides, there was no other way of waiting.

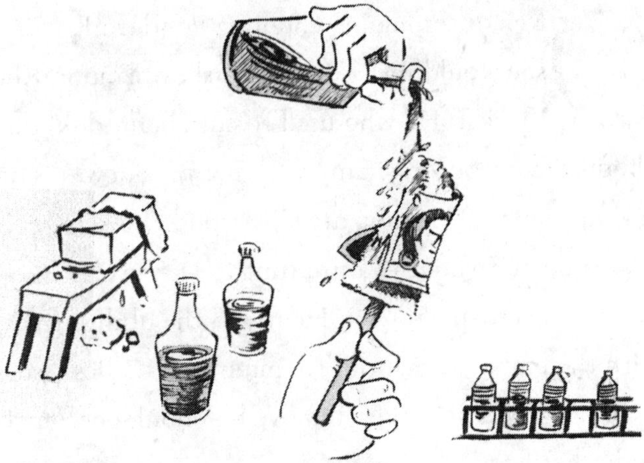

It was this day that she would find freedom from her beauty. It was this face which had made her a fugitive from thousands of eyes. The palms which took the heat from her face would heave and she'd diffuse into a fog of colour. To be born in Greater Kailash, to have such a complexion, she was fed up of listening to such things.

If you like my appearance, my colour so much, then cover it under a hundred other colours—hearing her say this, he stood there, quietly.

Often, after having chaat at Pandara Road, she would insist on eating shawarma in Khan Market. He who used to eat chuda-dahi and bhaat-achaar began sitting with her on sidewalks and eating prawns. When he ate Chettinad chicken for the first time at Swagath Restaurant in Defence Colony, he became crazy about it. He found the ability to deal with the embarrasment of sitting in the Ladies' Seat. Now he would no longer remove his shoulder from under her head...

Blue jeans from Levis and a white t-shirt from Crocodile. Both were happy at having bought them from South Ex. Under the 85-foot-tall statue of Shiva, he tore open the Mother Dairy packet with his teeth. She started offering the milk at Shiva's feet. In her Tag sunglasses, he spotted the Aghori sadhu staring. He smashed the coconut in such anger that she let out a little scream.

Oops, just ignore no. We're here to be spiritual, not violent. Shiva will take care of him.

Magadh Express, Bogey number S-1.
Returning from Delhi to Patna, when I saw Bernard Shaw in her hands I just slunk out of there. It looked like she would be an English show-off. I roamed around in the other bogeys looking for a girl reading Premchand. When I'd come from Patna, there had been so many girls with even a *Grah Shobha* in their hands. Thinking of all this, I started reading my copy of poor old Colonel Ranjit.
Loafers have their own special language problem!

Not even a single flyover has been built in the city yet and you've already given up on the Taant sari?

But you're still wearing that cheap Bagh Chaap kurta. Like the yellow taxis of Kolkata. People have been roaming around in Boleros and Sumos for ages now.

Ya I know...I saw Monali yesterday, in the Maniktala Pandal. Incredibly stunning!

Achha, so I'm being wrapped up in a Taant while Monali is incredible. This difference between liking and looking comes from that exact place in your head where there's a button for looking at girls. You could've just gone with Monali!

A car stuck in a traffic-jam and inside the car, their fight. Right then some boys start dancing at the roadside pandal...Julie-Julie, Johnny ka dil tujhpe aaya Julie, tu hi to meri jaan hai-jaan hai...(Julie-Julie, Johnny has lost his heart to you Julie, You're my life-my life...)

The passion wrought by the Yezdi bike was such that as soon as he sat astride the Pulsar she started to fly like Rati Agnihotri and he began to fly her like Kamal Hasan. The retro magic of old films spread in his dreams. He began hanging around the shops outside Kamala Nehru College for hours. But the girls stepping out through those gates hadn't even seen *Ek Duje Ke Liye*. Their Vasu began running loans at the shops. Waiting for someone, he drowned in debt...

Khap, Somewhere Around Us

Why is this guy in the blue coat standing with that book clutched to his chest? To remain lost in such questions during their precious moments of love was her habit. That was why he remained quiet. He let his fingers lose themselves in her hair. His increasingly restless breathing began to encounter everything Ambedkar used to say about creating a world without caste—just you wait, that very book is going to bring us together forever. These two eyes, they can see so much, no? Yes, a lot.

In Lakshmanpur Bathe too, a pair of eyes is seeing everything. For a long time now, they've been keeping count of all those who see them once but never again.
Uff, your mind, no, it's become a Facebook status.
Here's me trying to see Delhi through your eyes and you're...
Yes, and I'm busy moving aside bed-sheets, reading brand names of mattresses...

The Rajkumar of Raja Garden began writing a letter. Not to his Mistress of Malviya Nagar but to the city Chief of Police—it's an appeal to his lordship that he must postpone loving in this city.

The horsemen of Raisina Hill, just to spoil the image of the lovers, have dumped Mobil Oil under every tree. The lovers, returning home late in the evening, have started being identified by the Mobil. As soon as this news hit the airwaves, a perfect storm hit the world of the lovers. The Vizier made his move and landed up in Bareilly. A statement was made from there that

everyone should stick to their work.

The Mistress of Malviya Nagar had been picked up from the Big Boss set and dumped in the hospital. It had been a good day for the Chief of Police. Without a case ever being registered, the Romeos had confessed. Not to keep going but to break it off...

Shouting slogans at Jantar-Mantar, they came close to each other. It seemed as if love had found the motive of life. Stricken by the terror of their parents, they were swaying in joy here. After three days, when they saw their middle-class parents in that crowd, they ran away. She was cursing Anna now. As they ate ice-cream at India Gate, their grand vision of changing the country turned to strategizing to quickly reach home.

Both of them knew that their families never went to temples except during the Navratras. Which is why every morning she would come from Rohini to Chattarpur. He would come from Gurgaon. Walking in the caves here, making wishes for each other, they were needlessly converting their affection into devotion. At each turn in the dark cave, he would pretend to stop, she would pretend fear. Touch was like that blessing in whose search they'd roam in temples...

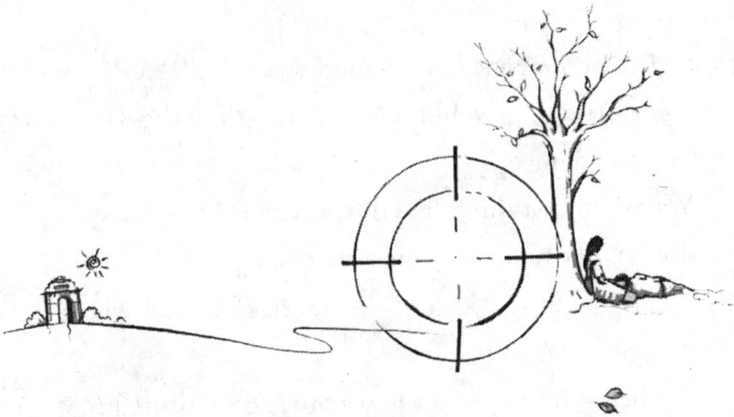

The trees of India Gate are such cons. They burn our backs even under their shade. The temperature is 44.1 degree Celsius.

And when did we ever decide that we'd change our plans for romance according to the weather!

Your head is all safe under the dupatta, I'm the one getting beheaded here.

Banta-Cold Drinks are all useless. Let's run away from this India Gate. Tomorrow's newspaper will print our picture, I'm telling you. See, they are searching for sun-burnt couples, see that TV guy.

Come, let's go out of focus...

I wish someone like Obama was a Collector in our district. He would have destroyed all the Khaps in one night.

Yes, when you think like this, it seems like a sweet dream. But remember once there's a gun in his hand, even Obama speaks just like a terrorist. Then where will you run?

I've heard he can see even when it's dark at night. Come no, let's do something for democracy from tomorrow morning. Till when will we keep hiding under the mango and peepal trees? Even when a jamun falls, it seems like some Khap's bullet has just hit us...

The first time they met, it was in an Aggarwal Sweets. Which is why she'd sometimes call him Dhoda and sometimes Gulab Jamun. They made this red shop-sign the nameplate for their love. The Khap guys started keeping watch on the many Aggarwal Sweets of the city. They began to meet in Nathu Sweets Corner of Sundar Nagar now. She no longer called him by the names of the sweets. When asked, she just said, that place was ours, this place is strange. Now only your name is trust.

O Bela, you've become Trinamool's, not Pablo's... neighbourhood love has been sacrificed at the altar of the Parties. There must be some Gud ka Sandesh left between us. I still carry the promise of that sari from the Dakhinapan emporium as debt. Will we never meet again, even if just so I can pay this off? Even if we cannot chat on Facebook because of the fear of Didi, you can at least come to Maniktala in a burkha. I cannot bear this terror anymore, Bela—
Yours, Pablo the poet, Pablo...

At midnight, Pablo's email came on the smartphone. Bela began to tremble. He's mad! Didn't become a poet but will get me killed by Neruda's name. First of all he falls in love with a Trinamool worker, then has the gall to send emails! When he did not recieve a reply, Pablo began sending one email after another. Bela would delete them from the inbox, then delete them from the trash. Then Biswas from the Cyber Cell began calling. Bela shivered, again. Right then, the birds on the Salt Lake trees made a clamour. Bela left her house and ran. The smartphone was still ringing. Pablo's name began to flash.

You're mad, Pablo, why did you send the email?
Why are you running, Bela?
I'm running to go throw this phone into Salt Lake. If they see the email, then!
Bela...you don't know...no one can run away from emails. No one can leave them behind.
Then, Pablo, why don't you run?

Dear Pablo, I remember you like the biryani at Aminia. In the test between love and politics, I have chosen politics. Whenever I smell biryani, Pablo, you always cross my mind, but with the memory of the thirty-four years of Left terror, I become like Didi. The politics of change cannot be done by changing sides. Pablo, our love has become like the chicken bharta at the Punjabi dhaba. I do remember you but Biswas from Cyber Cell follows me like a shadow. We cannot change our Parties, can we not change our love either? I'm like muri-bhaja now. Pablo, do you want love or the Party? I'm not asking you, I'm asking myself. What do I want? Pyaar or Party?

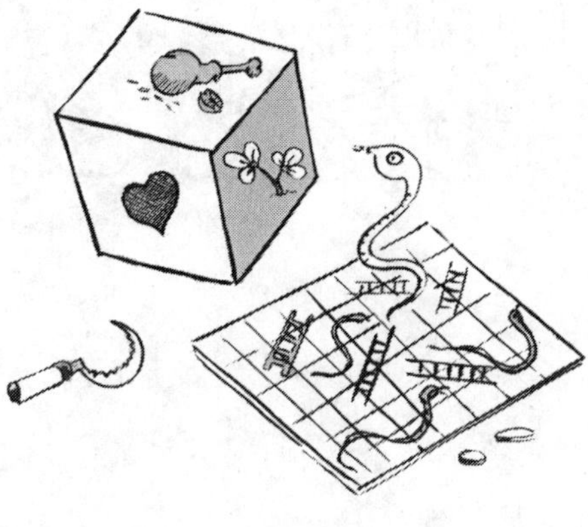

Give It All You've Got, Life!

The conversation was over. To call it incomplete was only an excuse.

You know, the dust that rises after these rallies raises no fear of a storm.

You're right. As soon as this dust clears, you and I, like these flyers strewn around, will be tossed this way and that.

So where will we meet now? Will you say or should I find out...

Do that, but if it's a ground like this Ramleela, that would be great.

Why? Yaar, I like politics during our breaks.

What I mean is, are we in love or in politics?

We're nowhere.

Then?

We're in Delhi, darling. What difference does it make where we meet!

We are living in a clean time. That has been cleaned out even before being cleaned up. Just say it clearly, what do you want to say...

Actually, it's not that I am coming clean or anything that I have to say it clearly.

Then just say what you have to say.

I said it no, not saying anything at all will clear things up.

So what are you saying, darling?

That we call spreading trash 'saying something'. If even two moments of silence get cleaned out in love, then what'll remain? Clean skies or trash?

100 per cent true. I swear by you.

But truth is truth. What is 36 per cent or 74 per cent? And why are you talking in percentages? Isn't our love 100 per cent?

But since the limit for disinvestment in truth has been increased, my love is no longer mine.

What?

Yes. We've all been disinvested.

If truth is not 100 per cent true, then it is not truth at all. Truth and love are not only meant for you, you know. They are for the borders of the country and for progress as well.

Listen.

Say.

You've gone crazy. Just shut this Facebook. We'll dream without disinvestment.

But I was only talking about life...

Do you know that you're happy for 20 per cent of the day and sad for about 12 per cent? For 10 per cent of the time, your mood is None Of The Above. And at least 8 per cent of that 'NOTA' is due to me...

Darling, are you watching me or the channel's survey?

O my dearest loser, you can either watch the TV or you can watch the moon...

Michelle, you know this victory, right. We've arranged for this applause for the sake of our own little peace. Why don't I take you in my arms and throw a photograph of our embrace into the thunder of this applause.

Yes, Barack, who has ever been able to change the future of the masses, at least the masses have changed our fate. I don't know when we were just fine, was it when we were the masses ourselves or now that we've become the rulers.

Yes, Michelle, you're right. This celebration of our victory is only ours. The rest have just come to dance. Let them dance, no! It's only a matter of a picture. You in my arms and I in yours.

Yes, yes, Barack, America's democracy is just a nice picture, like this picture of you and me.

Hmm, this guy who writes LaPreKs doesn't know this, does he!

What?

That our love is only a picture.

The Sector 4 crossing has been witness to so many false promises being mounted or taken down. One day we too shall be hung in a hoarding here. Vaishali does not wait for its nagarvadhu, its city-bride. The builder who made this Amrapali building made tons of money in the property deal. The city-bride carried her city on her shoulders and came from that Vaishali to this Vaishali. She is now asking for votes in the Corporation elections as Babbu Singh's bride. And what are you doing?
I'm just entering it in the records.
What, our dreams?
No, this crumbling neighbourhood, this Vaishali.

Listen, have you registered on JailChalo.com yet? You'd heard no, about when Dada ji went to jail following Gaanhi baba's orders.

Ya...Even my dad's friends had gone to prison with JP.

Oh, really!

God kasam, no ya...My dad was an Indira-bhakt. Actually he liked the Emergency. He was against Lalu from the beginning.

Oh, that way.

But this time, let's go together. JailChalo.com is cool na!

Ya, ya, very cool.

Then my dude, come, let's go to jail. Anna taught us our first steps on the Dot Com, now we shall walk right into jail for country and community .

Listen:...you'll be with me, no...I mean...you won't ditch...

Uff...what the hell are you saying...Of course I'll go to jail with you...We are together for ever...

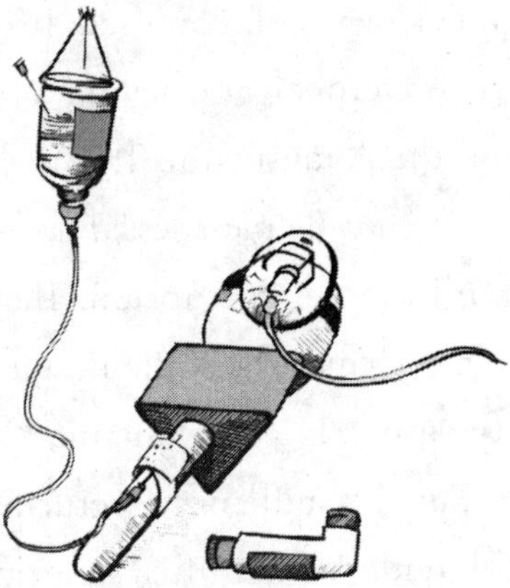

The breeze debates with the silent leaves, no! Shut up. Your brain is stuffed with all the junk of anchoring. Even the breeze is debating!

Yes, I'm like that. Why are you being angry? Let me finish what I'm saying or should I take a break? During the break my questions go take a bath with Lux or Liril and then come back swaggering about in Dora Vests.

Uff, this anchor has turned into a Romeo! Listen, can't you leave TV?

No, it's a lung disease. It will leave me, I won't leave it.

Shut up, you jinx.

September seems all confused. It's either impatient to get to October or grieving at having left behind the August rain. The air has a strange sort of heat, or that helplessness a government gets in the face of inflation or corruption. They were sitting under the palm tree in the Millennium Park and pulling at the grass. He kept patting her back, gently blessing her but the smile never returned to their faces. The mungfali guy also left after shouting a few times. The waste-picker kid watched them closely for a while and thought, what strange lovers! Neither do they talk nor do they leave the grass alone. If only lovers like this visit the park the gardener's job is as good as gone!

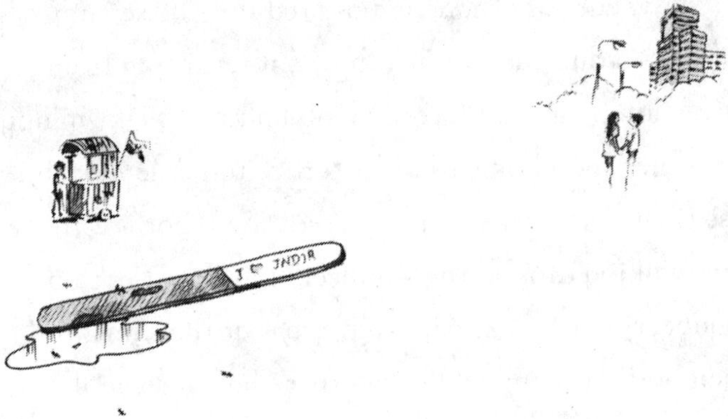

Both their lips were stuck to the Choco Bar. This fun of dividing the ice-cream and licking it together in the middle of the crowd, it was all due to Anna. As the hunger-strike was called off and the crowd started dispersing, their little seclusion evaporated into thin air. If only the strike had stretched to another week.

With a heavy heart they returned to Barakhamba, and turned once again to look at Ramleela Maidan.

See it for as long as you like, it's in the shadow of this crowd that we've shared a few moments of the protest. I can do anything for India, really, but now I don't know when the next hunger-strike is...

The eyes of exhaustion are red like the setting sun and the feet, aching, as if returning from a long journey. A settled job had never shown any way other than home to office, office to home. For the first time, even if it was just to see Anna, both of them kept walking around the Ramleela Maidan. Kept on sloganeering till late. After ten years at the same job, when both of them held each other's hands, even if it was just to save themselves from the from the jostling of the crowds, it all felt like that first time, when for this same chance, they'd keep hesitating to cross the street. Suddenly, a car speeding towards them had given them the chance.

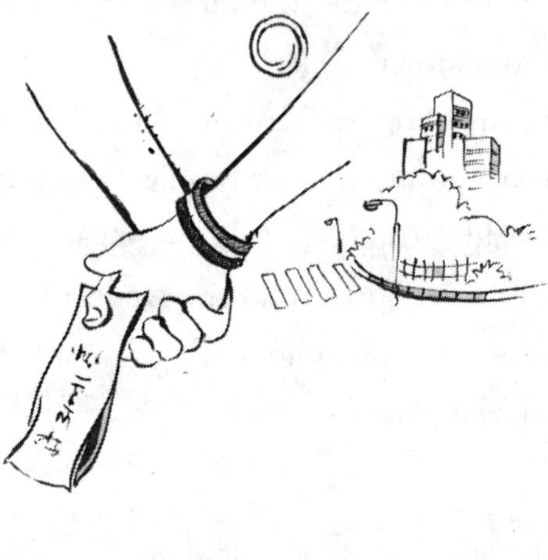

While passing through Shanti Path, I don't know why everything seems so grand! The 620 bus from Munirka, before it reaches Teen Murti, seems to pass through a European spring. At the window seat at the back, our shoulders brushing against each other's brush against the lines of a poet. I wish, sometimes, we could feel all those cotton-soft instances of touch. Oblivious to the whistle of the conductor, which song do you get lost in? Who is there with you in that song from *Silsila*...

You know, last night in my dream, both Anna and Gandhi turned up.

Come on, yaar! You've become very political. Relax. Why don't I ever turn up in your dreams? Sometimes it is Sitaram's article, another time it is Sandip Pandey's. Just stop! Look at that bougainvillea, isn't it beautiful. Even the air of JNU seems violet. Shall we take the 615 to Janpath?

No, I don't want to go to Jantar Mantar.

With the speed of light, their dreams started circling the planets. Abandoning all sorts of revolutions in the middle just to search for a place to love had not only made them bourgeois but had also turned them into deserters. How can a metro station be called Kalkaji Mandir, such questions had stopped making their blood boil. As soon as the Chattarpur station came, she bowed her head towards the temple and he looked towards his favoured god. A little journey has turned out to be so long!

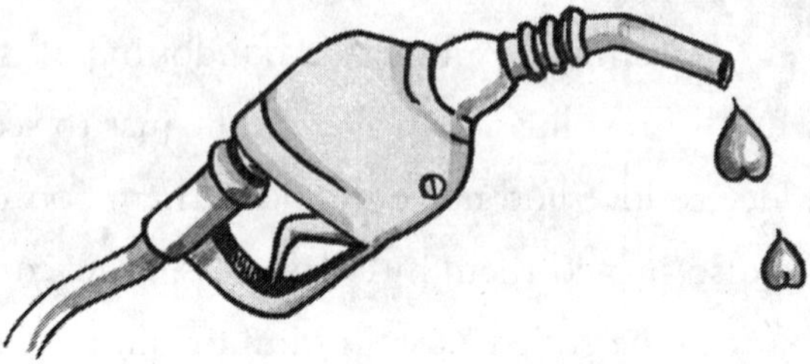

Darling, let us meet just once a week now. In any case, I'm dead tired driving around looking for a place to meet. What should we do in this heat? Let's take a little summer break. Anyway, petrol's five rupees costlier from tomorrow. You know, you also need to get out of your house a bit. At least take a bus till ISBT.

Arre yaar, the price of petrol goes up, and you eat my head! I won't come, okay. Then don't say you miss me.

This time, we won't go to Ramleela. We'll go to Chaupati. We'll crash against the waves of the sea. We'll get tired, then rest at Azaad Maidan. We will walk down these roads, each as long as a lifetime. We'll do our bit for the 11 lakh rent of the MMRDA grounds. We will shout Anna-Anna. And then when the noise rises, we'll shout I love you-I love you instead. If in the place of this Lokpal, we can have a Lovepal, then it is a good day for us lovers. How great will that be. At Humayun's Tomb, we won't pretend to sleep in each other's laps.

Now It's Your Turn

Some years ago, I had the opportunity to sketch for one of the books of the popular Hindi writer Nirmala Jain... In it, she'd said that 'after a point, any city becomes a way of life for those living in it, like we construct the city, the same way it starts constructing us...and we start being called Dilli walahs, Agra walahs or Mumbai walahs.' While drawing for *The City Happens in Love* I could understand these things in greater depth. 'Why are the gardeners of Lodhi Gardens sad during autumn... Even the deserted streets and lanes shelter so many hopes' Reading these lines, I felt like LaPreK was for me. With every passing page, this feeling made a home in me that I don't need someone else's lenses to see this city. It is precisely the speciality of the way Ravish writes that I didn't even know when, from the illustrator of this book, I became its author. How successful my attempt has been, this only the reader will tell, but I'm grateful to Ravish. He gave me that freedom and a kind of kinship. While working on the book, my respect for him has grown even more. As far as the format, shape and the practicality of this book was concerned, Satyanandji's guideline about the 'eye of the fish' was admirable. Along with this, I'm grateful to the Managing Director of Rajkamal Prakashan, Mr. Ashok Maheshwari, who gave me this opportunity.

People's attachment to a book is its success. I too, during the making of this book, have made a thousand little niches for myself or cleared the ones I had of their webs...now it's your turn...

18 January 2015 VIKRAM NAYAK
New Delhi

Translator's Acknowledgements

More than a hundred people responded with full enthuness when I asked for help in translating Ravish's book title. Comment after comment on that thread helped me untie the beautiful but Gordian knot of *Ishq Mein Shahar Hona*. I don't know whether we've been able to capture the staggering beauty and the many meanings of the name that Ravish chose for his book but, in my estimation, *A City Happens in Love* comes the closest.

I owe Niranjan Pant ten treats, or twenty, for his suggestion of 'To Be a City in Love'. It was as smart as they come. It broke my heart not to be able to take Supriya Nair's absolutely slick suggestion of 'In Love I Became a City'. It had prompted the similar 'In Love We Became a City' which was damn apt for the two lovers that loiter on every page of this book. Biswamit Dwibedy's crisp 'Become a City in Love' stayed with me for a long time too.

Mangalesh Dabral, Maaz Bin Bilal, GJV Prasad, Nayana Dasgupta, Mohini Gupta, Onaiza Drabu,

Aditi Rao, Nabina Das, Rakhshanda Jalil, Siddharth N. Kanoujia, Aishwarya Iyer, Manash Firaq, Annie Zaidi, Riya Gupta, Smriti Nevatia, Shals Mahajan, Chaynika Shah, Mohit Satyanand, Ujjwal Bhattacharya, Aanchal Khulbe, Giti Chandra, Simona Sawhney, Ania Loomba and many, many others joined that conversation and helped me parse the many layers of the stunning name of Ravish's book. To each of them I owe gratitude.

Satyanand Nirupam of Rajkamal Prakashan and Anurag Basnet of Speaking Tiger were always helpful and encouraging.

The University of Iowa International Writing Program gave me the time and space to finish most of this translation.

Vqueeram Aditya Sahai, Dhiren Borisa, Dhrubo Jyoti, Aditi Rao, Anannya Dasgupta, Vebhuti Duggal, Sameer Chopra, Sandip Kuriakose and my colleagues at Ambedkar University Delhi helped in ways that count.

Dhrubo Jyoti, Benil Biswas, Hansda Sowvendra Shekhar and Kingsuk Dasgupta deftly explained the Calcutta references. Dhrubo replied to the late-night messages I sent him with one Bengali phrase or another. Pratyush Pushkar, who within seconds of asking, was forthcoming with a detailed definition of lafua. My college-mate Kadambari Mishra who gets a phone call from me once a year asking for a translation of this Bihari phrase or that. She has always indulged me. Ankita Anand cleared some doubts. Gautam Ghai, Ankush Gupta, Prateeq Kumar and Ratna Raman were all prompt with their various meanings for golabaaz.

To each of them I owe thanks.

July 2018,
New Delhi

AKHIL KATYAL